Ethereal Love

WRITTEN BY KID GILLIS

Ethereal Love

Written By:

© 2022 Kid Gillis

Published By:

© 2022 Years of Ages Productions

ISBN: 979-8-9862864-9-5

9 798986 286495

Dedication

To those who love hard and those who don't love at all. To those who are guarded and those who are open. To those who know love, life, triumphs, and trials. To those, I dreamt, created, built, did life with, loved, lost, and let down...

This is for you, for me, and for us. To our crazy past, present, and future; to our current healings, happenings, and maturing — It's all love, forever and always. I love you, regardless.

Table of Contents

Ethereal Love

Late

When I arrived, I was in a rush.

There was no time to catch my breath.

No time to stop or think.

I just had to get where I was going.

Where I was going, I had to get.

The early bird catches the worm.

But, around here – I was late, again.

Trip

Boarding a crowded train,

I fell into a stranger's arms.

Held in a warm embrace,

You placed me back onto my feet.

Introducing myself, apologizing;

You smiled bashfully, looking away.

And, without a word said; I could tell

You were happy to oblige my trip.

Mesmerized

Luckily, that would be

The last time I'd see you.

Although, I'd remember:

How you saw me blush,

How your eyes read my soul,

How your smile lit up a room,

And

How I felt within your arms...

Psyche

As I went on with my daily routine;

I became uneasy bumping into

    The idea of you, again.

You weren't the first person

    I had accidentally encountered.

But you were the first to leave

    Your imprint upon my psyche.

Elevators

I've never liked small spaces.

The constant ups and downs;

Being confined behind closed doors.

Waiting to arrive at destinations;

I've never been a fan of elevators.

Yet, here I am, patiently waiting;

Except this time,

    I was intrigued by the ride.

Something changed when you stepped in

    Before the doors closed;

Mere Stranger

There I was – minding my business; until I laid eyes upon you. At that moment, I realized – not even the wonders of the world could compare to your magnificence.

My lip quivered in fear as I observed your splendor. Your essence left me in awe as you walked across the floor, lighting up my darkened mind.

I grew still as adoration began to tug upon my forlorn heart, causing me to desire – all you had to offer, although you were just a mere stranger.

Hello & Goodbye

When you said "Hello."

I then said goodbye

To everything I used to know

Before you...

Invitation

Our smiles invited each other over;

Before, we decided to approach.

Our mouths didn't utter a word.

But, our eyes spoke.

Voicing everything for us...

Honey

Your name was

The purest honey I ever craved

    To taste upon my tongue;

While speaking,

You began to steal my attention,

    With your sugar-filled words.

Hungered,

I began to fall into

    My sticky imaginations.

Access

Though our time was short-lived

And our conversation was brief;

We opted to speak again, after

Exchanging information in the city's streets.

Old Fashioned

With a pen in hand,

I wrote my number upon your palm.

With your phone in hand,

You chuckled while intrigued.

Calling me old-fashioned.

Fate

Although we were eager to meet again;

It was hard to stop and allow fate

    To initiate the right timing;

Without our help,

Without our feelings being in the way,

    Or anything clouding our judgment;

Happening

Time flew by.

Life went on.

I continued living,

    While you continued being.

Days grew shorter.

Moments seemed longer.

Silence took over.

But, our minds screamed a little bit louder

    For something to happen for us...

Texts

Before speaking face to face again, we learned patience through short texts and long conversations. Understanding each other's tones and adjusting to one another's personalities, we explored reading between the lines while accepting the distance between us. From our words to our actions, we noticed something was beginning to form between us. Yet, we never mentioned it, just observed cautiously.

Waiting Game

When our time came to finally meet;

We took it without hesitation.

However,

I arrived too early and you, too late.

Leaving me waiting.

And you, rushing again.

Nervous

Approaching you,

My mind drew a blank when you arrived.
My heart raced. The muscles in my face hurt
from smiling as we embraced. I was so glad
to see you.

Tongue-tied and sweaty-palmed.

You opened your mouth to release the
butterflies felt but stumbled over your words
like a child with untied shoelaces. However,
I caught you, again – mid-fall.

Wide-eyed and blushing.

I stood kindled with curiosity, observing.
Inhaling, the breath of fresh air of which you
are – just as anxious. I was filled with the
same butterflies, trying to reach cloud nine
just from being in your presence.

I guess – we were nervous.

Existing

We stood, sizing up our judgments.

Unsure of If we should

Move on, letting go

Or

Continue being present at the moment.

See, as strangers –

We can be whoever we are right now.

And worry about becoming someone else,

Later on;

School Kids

With no plans or place to go, we roamed the city. Walking down unknown paths, we seized the moment and took in the scenery.

Unsure of what to say, we played the game of staring and then looking away like school kids. In all innocence and ignorance, we taunted each other while monkeying-around until we felt comfortable.

With laughter as loud as the music blaring from our phones, our conversation fell in sync with our stride and vibes. We found ourselves familiar, while visiting an old school yard.

 Swings

Life passed us by as we dwelt behind metal gates. We swung to and fro as our feet were treading along the rubber blacktop.

The world screamed aloud in urban tones; as we spoke of life's different pinnacles and the challenges we had to endure.

Nothing seemed to matter, really. Instead, we were captivated by each other's desire to fly and fear of falling. We considered our options by allowing the wind to guide us.

Depending solely on blind faith in the unseen and unexpected, we held on for dear life while soaring upon our dreams, trusting that rusted swing set wouldn't fail us.

Free Flow

Neither in a rush nor in a hurry;

We vowed to let go of our insecurities.

Excluding all of our expectations;

We adapted to the free flow of things.

Besides the vibe of our energies mixing;

And the guiding of our hearts' intentions;

We hoped to enjoy whatever we'd find

In the midst of this experience, together...

Once In Awhile

We conversed about crossing paths.

Joked about not searching for anything

    While wandering this world alone.

And for a moment, I realized;

I wasn't the only person who desired

    To be noticed or enjoy someone's

    Presence, once in a while.

Seasons

As months passed by,

We changed over time.

Together and apart;

Embracing our growth,

While forming a well-seasoned bond;

We became friends.

Close friends – very close friends.

Eyes

Looking into the windows of your soul,

    The only thing I noticed

    Was a radiant light shining forth

    Through your inner being.

That's what made me curious to know you.

It made me wonder who you were.

Gardens

Trading glimpses of our beings

    Through portions of our biographies;

We toiled the grounds of friendship.

Sharing embarrassing memories,

    Adding to our social followings;

We planted seeds of an instant connection.

Engaged in harmless interactions,

    At dinner in public places;

Over time, we established

    A garden of possibilities.

Before leaving and saying goodbye;

We found ourselves full of life,

    With fruit and butterflies.

    Thriving in our own type of paradise.

Noticed

Before we became,

We noticed.

Expression

You say the craziest things. But somehow, I understand what you are trying to convey, even without speaking.

Living

Time ceased to exist

When we're together;

We're often

Lost in the zone.

Taking 2 a.m. drives.

Breaking bread during rainstorms.

Singing off-key while dancing to

The beat of our own drumming.

Making classic memories.

Risking it all – living.

Just living in the moment.

Breaking Bread

Honestly,

I don't often share

My time with anybody

Or a seat at my table;

Yet, when it comes to you

I make an exception;

You're the only person

I'll share a moment with.

I guess that says a lot.

Doesn't it?

Butterflies

There are instants when I'm around you that I tend to stop and catch my breath. Bright-eyed and smiling, I'm fascinated by all that you are.

Leaning in closer, I'm attentive to every word that escapes your lips. Moving near, I yearn to be closer to you.

Yet, when you sing or laugh aloud, butterflies often take flight within the midst of my core. Causing me to behold heights I've only dreamt of experiencing but never experienced, alone.

Bonding

I told you stories of ancient. Names of people who gave me life. Occurrences that produced my history. Influences that left me strengthened. Memories that brought me delight.

You listened to what I said, taking notes, learning how you could care for me.

You told me stories of youth. Events that nurtured your inner being. Recollections that shaped your future. Family members that supported your dreams. Friends that gave and kept you rooted.

I listened to what you said, taking notes, learning how I could assist you.

Follow the Leader

When you called,

I came running.

Ready to go wherever,

You might lead us.

Train

You hate to travel, never knowing where to go. Directionally incompetent, you avoided the motions to move forward.

But when I grabbed your hand, leading you down into the darkness - you experienced a rush. While fear and anxiety heightened your excitement, our heartstrings tugged as we journeyed through tunnels to our new destination.

Arriving at the station, where we were first acquainted – our adventure began to unfold. And that's when I knew you'd remember the beginning of our trip, our incredible fall, and the terrifying feeling of uncertainty from the future's presence lurking afar off.

Person

Before my mouth could say it.

Before my mind could fathom.

My heart already knew.

You are my person.

Visual

You

See in me

All of the things

I cannot see in myself, yet.

Eyes of God

When I look into your eyes, heaven's gates are opened. And, I am welcomed home by the light of your grace.

I'm able to roam your streets at will. As if I am a forgiven saint, suddenly worthy of your gifts of forgiveness, love, and faithfulness.

Lord, have mercy on me. Forgive me; I can't help but worship you now. Never have I ever witnessed someone so beautiful.

My God, I can't believe you're real...

Reflection

You're the person

Who speaks my native language,

While holding a mirror

In front of yourself...

Audacity

You had the audacity

To walk into my life,

Making yourself at home

Growing, oh so comfortable.

Whatever

Suddenly, nothing mattered when I started and ended my days with you. It's like when you came around, I was ready for whatever might come my way.

Close

No, you aren't mine.

Yet, we're close like you are.

Late - Pt.2

As I ran through the station,

    Down the stairs, to the platform;

I was greeted by you holding the train door,

    And an empty seat;

One, which was right next to yours.

Creative Love

They said:

"Be careful, falling for a creative..."

I should've listened because you love making a beautiful mess out of things. As if the voids in my black and white world are in need of your colorfully chaotic pieces, but, honestly...I don't need them.

Yet, I still can't help but admire your perception and imaging. I'm a fan of how you address your brokenness boldly, paint the world with the brightest optimism, and bring to life that which was lifeless.

And perhaps, I'm in need of more of your vision, your love, your passion, and your most delicate fragments. They are beautiful, after all. I'm learning to love them and myself properly as I learn to love you.

Attachment

My heart is

Connected to your sleeve.

Every movement made,

I'm pulled in your direction.

And likewise,

You are also to mine.

Let Up

It's like when you showed up,

    You decided to never leave.

Gifting me with your constant presence.

Soon enough, I found myself consumed

    By the thought of you.

After a while,

    It was hard for me to let up.

Hide and Seek

We played

Hide and seek

With our emotions;

Although,

We knew

Everything was exposed,

Between us.

Feelings

I don't need you.

But, I want you.

I don't like you.

But I love you.

I don't say it.

And, neither do you.

We just know —

It is what it's supposed to be.

Crazy About You

The only pressure applied

Was the question about

When would be the right time

To reveal that:

I'm crazy about you...

take

I've been told:

"...It only takes a few minutes to like someone. It only takes a moment to fall. It'll only take a couple of months to be in love. It'll only take the best years of your life to experience forever with someone..."

And although this might sound crazy;

This is something I'm beginning to want.

Pursuit

You began to pursue me.

And, I began to let you.

God Sent

Every morning,

I received texts from you

Claiming:

      Blessings over our lives.

      Praises over our bond.

      Prayers over our day.

      Worship over our love.

Leaving me highly encouraged.

Hoping you're the one God sent.

Cafe

Hungered, we sat in the back of a café. Conversing over bagels and slow jams, we sat with coffee mugs covering smiles and napkins hiding outbursts of laughter.

Strangers watched from afar, noticing the crumbs of our conversations. Losing track of time, the world grew dark while we explored our differences.

The barista blushed as we mixed our cream and sugar with fascinations of hot chocolate-filled comforts and home-style hospitality.

Abandoning our table at closing, we scurried onto the frigid streets. Standing amidst the city lights, we vowed to meet again.

Before the stars left, our eyes and lips grew acquainted; we said goodnight. Forever changed, yearning for another moment in paradise.

First nor Last

This won't be

Our first

Nor will it be

Our last

Time, together.

Foundation

Our most embarrassing insecurities and reflections became the very things we liked about each other the most.

Those perfect imperfections, those weird and dorky quirks, those random gestures and doings, only a particular person could love;

Yeah, those simple things bonded us. That substance drew us in. Those were the things that became the foundation of our relationship.

ecor

After a while,

I found my heart ornamented

with your personal décor.

As if it had become

      Your new home,

      Your personal shrine,

      Or something...

Seeking

Being with you,

I found what I was seeking after.

    A glimpse of good.

    A spark of hope.

    A familiar image.

    A sign and wonder.

Understatement

You asked.

"What am I to you?"

I looked at you and smiled

As you mouthed "...a friend?"

I laughed, saying,

"Oh, my love,

That's an understatement

When it comes to you..."

Unknown

We craved

What our souls

Had never known,

Each other.

Supposedly

Supposedly, I am

Everything your heart desires.

Supposedly, I am

The one you envision yourself with.

Supposedly, I am

The one you've fallen for.

And, I suppose,

I'd have it no other way.

Supposedly,

Of course...

Titles

Do I have to ask or say?

(They say we have to label this)

You got me, and I got you.

(But we already know what it is)

I'm with you. You're for me.

(You're all that I want)

You're mine, I'm claiming.

(Enough said)

I need you, I want you, and I love you.

(I love you, regardless)

Regardless.

Expectations

Is it too good to be true?

Are fairytales real?

Am I in over my head?

Am I daydreaming again?

As time moved on,

We began to question things.

Because this was becoming

More than what we expected.

Hidden

There are things about you that I don't know.
There are things about me I dare not show.

The unknown, we choose to avoid every
time we cross its path as we try to get where
we're going. When backed against a wall,
we speak in foreign riddles. Our native
tongue changes as our souls retreat back to
that unknown dwelling.

We've hidden our castle and crowns within
the depths of the unknown's forest. Hoping
to die on its hills, praying its barriers will
protect and hide us from our invaders. But,
the time has come for us to let our guard
down.

Yet, we don't know how to do it - to step out
of our darkness, escape the forest, and accept
our peers and ourselves, alike.

Insecurities

Our insecurities,

Forced us to examine ourselves;

And, question everything else around us...

Many Souls

With you,

I'm in liking.

With you,

I'm in love.

But I'm still not sure −

What to think of this affection.

Because I have loved many souls.

Yet, never committed to any of them.

The Soul Quest

When asking about soulmates, I began to listen as you revealed what you believed. That love often comes in various forms, through multiple persons, at different moments in time, when needed.

When asked about previous loves, you became vague as we conversed about the moments that made you rise and fall, that stole your heart, and knocked the breath out of your lungs;

When speaking, you brushed it off. As if you've never had someone set your core ablaze or somehow forgot your quest for love...

xperience

We're from different ages.

Yet, wisdom has derived from my voyage through time. I've observed enough to know what to do and how to get by.

We're from different places.

But, your journey has given you experience. Hands-on learning and lessons taught through living have equipped you to take on the world.

We're different.

Still, we dare not try to contend with each other's past. But, we try our best to create a future the two of us could only dream of experiencing together.

Walls

If I let my guard down, there's no telling what will come from behind these walls of mine.

If I let you in, there's no telling what would happen after you get a glimpse of my insane reality.

If I let my guard down,

If - I let my guard down...

Remember

Let's not pretend we don't have a past.

The old memories are imprinted in our minds. The names of lost loves are engraved on our hearts. Even the images of others that are still touching our souls;

Admit it...You remember.

How could you forget? A pure heart never disremembers. Because real love is hard to find without a trace of – faults, regrets, or recollections of those you miss.

Risky Business

We're risking it all.

Sacrificing so much of ourselves,

To develop a connection with each other.

Worthy

I often wonder

If I am worthy

To be given such

Affections.

Baggage

I've learned to carry myself well. Everything was presented impeccably. There's not a moment you'll see me a mess.

Everything is tucked in and strategically placed. I am clean cut and hot pressed. No one has seen another as swift.

But there are times when I am alone...I become undone in the worst way. Stripped bare; Pure flesh and raw emotions.

I let it all hang out as I try to grasp reality and its challenges, amongst other things I'm carrying inside of me.

Whole

Perhaps, some hidden parts of me are unlovable. The parts of me that are invisible. The ones locked away in the darkest chambers. Those lying dormant inside of me and my heart;

Those parts of me are special, sacred even. But, most wouldn't understand or accept those pieces. So, they never resurface once buried deeply. Not a glimpse of my shattering is seen by the naked eye of strangers who lack love's reflection.

Only those like me, who also carries around a void. Those hoping to be noticed by beautiful souls for all the right reasons because that which is broken can only be fixed by the love of them who can see them as whole...

Inner Being

If I let my guard down; If I let you in – into my world, my heart, my being...will you be able to handle it, or will you run away as soon as I introduce you to the real me? That's the unanswered question that scares me...

Consideration

I love you.

But I think we should call it quits.

Before we start something,

That'll have a tragic end...

Explore

We can go back to the beginning.

Forgetting everything known.

At any given moment, we can start over.

Single and lonely but never alone.

However, that's not what I want.

We are something I want to explore...

Fearful

I'm not fearful of who you were.

I'm not afraid of who you are.

Nor am I frightened by

Whom you're bound to become.

Because I know you;

Wants, Needs, and Desires

If this isn't what you want,

Voice what you need.

Whatever you desire,

Will be honored here.

But, leave your fears behind.

Let go of the expectations

Of what can go wrong.

And embrace what you are truly after.

Buried Treasure

Questions began to arise as we dove into deeper waters. The darkness I was afraid of began to surround us quickly.

Yet, we swam closer to the ocean floor, seeking each other's treasured soul, without knowing how to swim well.

Risking it all, to find what we were looking for...

Rescue

If we fall too fast or sink too deep;

And, you let go of me

In the midst of the waves,

For however long it takes,

I'll hold my breath in search of you;

Because I know at the moment,

I can't be without you.

Open

Since nothing was off limits between us,

We expressed ourselves openly.

Without lacking conversation,

We told each other everything.

A few Things

It's easy to pretend.

Even more so, to lie.

However, you've forced me

To do a few things:

    To open up.

    To love.

    To trust.

    And to live my truth.

Alive

In a short period of time,

You took hold of me,

Showing these old soul and bones

What it means to live and be alive...

Choices

During our most difficult days, we learned how to be present. How to praise each other for the small things. How to support each other through successes and losses. How to push and motivate each other during the hardships. And how to finish everything else together.

Wounded

Falling harder, we began to notice

    The delicate pieces

    Of our souls that ached.

The wounds we had, which hadn't healed.

    And the baggage

    We hadn't unpacked yet.

Allowance

I can only do for you,

What you will allow,

When you'll allow me to actually do it.

I can only do for you,

What you will allow,

When you'll allow yourself to actually do it.

Surgery

Opened,

Our hearts lay exposed, before us, beating.

Curious,

We explored the hidden chambers

With every question asked of us.

Understanding,

We flat-line while being resuscitated,

As we continue to dig deeper.

Trying our hardest

To make each other better

By healing what's ailing within us.

Drawn

You're a person of little words.

You twiddle with a pencil in hand.

Sketching, present moments

    Into a book of depicted memories.

Hoping to somehow salvage the past

    For all its good.

And, treasure your present days

    With all it's worth.

This is why I'm in awe of all you do.

You're picture perfect.

And, I'm drawn to you.

Storm Chaser

You feel strongly,

Like a storm brews inside you.

And the only way to release it,

Is by sending your world

Into a whirlwind.

And, I'm just a storm chaser.

Intrigued by how you process.

Curious to know how powerful you are

Even after,

All the damage is done.

Super Hero

Your obsession with saving everyone,

Often reveals

You have a golden heart and a dark past

You never speak of.

Survival

Darling, you can't find a reason to get out of character because you've been innocent throughout your life. It must be nice to only have to worry about experiences instead of survival. But unfortunately, all of us don't have such a privilege.

Past

Honey,

Your past doesn't make you

Any less valuable or worthy

Of this love,

I will continue to give you, regardless.

Unconcerned

Revealing bits of my former days, you don't
bat an eyelid at the horrid details or stories.
Even while blushing a million shades of red
while opening up, you remind me of all the
memories we're going to make together...

More

Damn,

We're slowly becoming

Less of ourselves and somehow,

A little bit more like each other.

Fear of Falling

I'm falling.

And that's the terrifying part.

Not your perfect imperfections.

But the new condition of my heart.

I think I need you

More than you need me.

And that's the scariest feeling

I've ever felt.

Sweetened

No guilt or shame.

I crave all that you are.

There's nothing hidden.

Nothing to add or take away;

You are literally:

    Blood and bones,

    Sweetened with the purest love;

Surely,

    Everything,

    I never knew I wanted or needed.

Tempted

Your lips

Caught my attention

As my brain

Screamed to kiss you;

So, I did it.

Fearless

You've become even more fearless

As time moved on;

As if the worst had already happened

And the best was yet to come.

One plus One

For some, there are many.

But,

For others, there is only one.

Radiant

The light radiating through you – from the inside and out; always catches my eye.

I can't help but wish upon the star of which you are; hoping for my wildest dreams to come true, after all;

Pressure

I tend to push you a little harder.

Hoping you'll never bend under pressure.

Yet, become more flexible when needed.

However,

I hope you'll never break

Because of me.

Vulnerable

Before we build upon this foundation.

Before we renovate our lifestyles.

Are you willing?

Are you able to sacrifice everything?

Have you truly counted the cost?

How vulnerable will you become?

Are you prepared for true love?

Before we give in,

Are you ready to open up?

Sunflower

Honey, I am intrigued by how you move within this world. You're a light chaser, always following the sun wherever it may go. How beautiful you are, maturing in your own rotation, blooming at the right pace, my lovely sunflower.

Euphoria

When I gaze into your eyes

I'm lost within the midst of you.

I'm on my own psychedelic trip

Of your euphoric soul,

High off your essence;

Inside Out

You're Beautiful, inside and out.

And, I don't have to remind you.

Because you confidently reflect it,

Without needing anyone's

Reassurance or validation;

Fandom

It doesn't matter how

Good or bad - you do.

You will always find me:

    Cheering you on as loud as I can,

    Throwing confetti – celebrating,

    Appreciating your effort,

    Assisting with guidance or help,

    Waiting to witness your next move.

Simply because I'm your number one fan.

Pieces

As we lay here together,

I can't help but take in:

    The beauty within your broken soul.

    The pain within your heart of love.

    And the darkness within

        Your illuminated mind.

So many pieces of the persona,

Making up your whole, beautiful self.

Person like You

I want it.

This dream you speak so fondly of.

This masterpiece you've created of love.

Honestly, I do.

I crave commitment.

I long for freedom, too.

But do I deserve it?

Do I deserve a person like you?

Prayers

In our most silent moments,

We both scream aloud.

The loudest love songs and

The most heart-wrenching prayers,

About each other, out of love...

Tell Em

What's the worst that can happen?

All you have to do is

Say it.

What are you so afraid of?

All you have to do is

Tell 'em.

First and Last

I want to take

My time with you,

Producing a couple

Of firsts and lasts.

All In

I'm giving all that I have.

Although, it isn't much;

But it's all that I got.

And I'm willing to part with it.

    For myself,

    And

    For you,

    Alone.

I Love You

Honey, I think...I love you.

And that's not easy for me to admit. I don't randomly throw these words around, hoping someone else would understand or catch feelings.

But, I mean them. I feel them. I see them – inside myself and you. But it's complicated. And, I'm anxious at the thought of telling you the truth.

But, when I think of you...powerful words come to mind. Love, forever, time...seems to slow down when you're around.

And, I become undone in your presence because I want to get to know you better. I want to be a part of your world. I want to build forever with you.

But I know I'm probably getting ahead of myself. So excuse me; if this is overwhelming...I know it's a lot to take in.

But honey, I think...I love you.

So, now that you know...can we talk about it? Can we discuss how to move forward? Or should we just leave things like this – unspoken? I'm cool with whatever you want to do.

Pretend

What was said can't be unsaid.

What was given can't be taken back.

What was seen can't be unseen.

What just happened, happened.

There's no need to make-believe.

I can't pretend it didn't occur.

Approval

We opened our homes like our hearts.

Becoming vulnerable amongst

Each other's families and friends.

Your parents loved me.

Your siblings adored me.

Your friends liked me, too.

And their approval is the biggest

Blessing I could have received;

Rather than your heart, of course.

Just Us

We've become that couple who's:

> Quarreling over where to park.

> Indecisive about where to eat.

> Forever on the go together.

> Sharing quick glances in silence.

> Completing each other's

>> Thoughts and sentences.

> Stealing each other's clothes.

> On the phone with nothing to

>> Say but refuses to hang up.

> Not giving a care about

>> Anything or anyone, just us...

Leap of Faith

If I asked you a question...

Would you simply tell me "...Yes!"

Or will you need time to think

About all the possibilities

That could happen instead?

Scribbles

I admit it.

I tend to scribble

My first and your last name

Upon pages of my notebooks...

Vows

Darling, I want all of you.

Everything you have to offer.

The best of you.

The worst of you.

The unsure and

The unknown, as well.

Leave out nothing.

Give me all that you are and have.

I will keep you.

I will care for you.

I will love you.

I will support you.

Beloved, I will be

Everything you want and need.

Don't hold back from me.

Because I'm all in.

Special

You are something special.

You speak to the spirit within me. You lift me up when I'm downcast. You cover me when I'm exposed. You honor me as I am.

I share myself, the part of me that is hidden. My heart is entirely unguarded. My wounds, bleeding while healing. I hold back nothing.

You've become more than a friend to me.

Your being - is the biggest blessing. Your presence – Captivating my attention. Your body – such beautiful gifting.

And, I know better than to get caught up or rush things...but I can't help how I feel about you.

You're special to me...

Day One

One day, you'll turn around. I'll walk towards you with a smile on my face. You'll take me by the hand and have me stand beside you. You'll promise me forever. I'll vow to always love you.

You'll ask if I mean it. I'll respond, "I do." I'll ask if you mean it. You'll respond, "I do." And, as we kiss, sealing the most significant moment of our new lives... We'll remember.

We always had feelings for each other. We always made each other smile. We always wanted the best for one another. We always walked the extra mile. We always covered each other. We always stood by each other side. We always loved one another. We always prayed about – This, Us, Love. We knew this day would come ever since day one.

Keys

As I handed you the keys to my heart

And our new home,

I might have slipped my entirety

Onto your ring as well...

Breath of Life - Pt.1

Give me a reason,

To exhale

Acceptance;

While you begin

To Inhale,

Freedom.

Control

Before I allow you

To take control,

Show me why

You should lead.

The Perfect Love

Bare my energy within your body. Wrap my language of love around your bones. Hide my truth within your heart. Keep my secrets within your soul.

And, when you've grown, full beyond capacity – become undone in my presence. Releasing all you have inside. Bypassing your guarded walls. Allowing entry to your purest form. Connecting me to your naked self.

Empty your body of what does not fulfill you while forgetting the past. Accepting the present. Appreciating new pleasures, while healing what's hurting and ailing, to receive and restore the simplicity of true love's perfection.

Breathe

I can hear you breathing.

Gasping while speaking;

You're trying to remain in control,

Losing grip because of new extremes,

Be unashamed,

Let out what you're holding in,

Come alive for me,

Breathe, Breathe, Breathe...

BREATHE!

taste

Your lips taste like

All of my guilty pleasures

And unjustifiable happenings...

Speak

I want to

Feel

Every word you

Say

Through every breath you

<u>Take</u>

Why don't you

SPEAK

Creating

Although,

You're a person

Of little words;

Your body,

Speaks a sacred language

Of creation.

Experienced

This life we chose;

It stretched and pushed us.

It caused us to rise and fall.

We experienced things together,

We never witnessed apart.

Awakened

I saw your stars within my darkness.

Tiny glimmers of hope aligned.

Stories of future happenings and history

Being brought together;

I looked in your direction, asking:

"When dawn comes with its skies ablaze,
will I still have your heart when I rise?"

Because, love was awakened before morning

In the midst of one of the darkest nights...

Unspoken

The glares we give each other,

Knowingly reveals

What our mouths can't say;

But, our minds express

Without hesitation...

Forever Young

I pray we never lose

What makes us young;

    The spark.

    The glow.

    The heat.

    The signal.

    Nor the flames –

        That keeps our fire going.

Even when we're at odds with each other...

Individuals

We continued to learn

How to be individuals,

While existing together...

Watched

Unfortunately,

People watched us

From afar.

Hoping

To see us

Rise and fall,

Come and go,

Crash and burn.

Remain

Some claim we're whipped.

Some claim we're too far gone.

Honestly, we're just trying to

Find the right pace to keep ahold of us;

While trying to gain balance in life

And remain our natural selves,

Amongst one another...

In Sync

The more we listened to others, the less we heard one another. Our heartbeat fell out of rhythm, as did the free flow we learned to cherish.

Honestly, I didn't know if it was possible to be in sync again. Our playlist changed our love song, which never sounded as it once did. And, in the process, our senses changed with our tune;

We went through the motions, trying to find our groove. But we didn't get the swing of things. Lines were crossed by accident, and toes were stepped on by err; as we danced around the problems in the rooms we shared.

Unaware of how loud everything and everyone had got. We couldn't grasp how silent we were while growing apart...

Rubbed

What didn't bother us before;

Slowly began to rub us the wrong way.

Causing us even more friction

Within the midst of our flame.

Diamond

Appealing, you are

Yet, modest in stature.

Rare, you are

Yet, valuable and worthy.

Simply, you are

A diamond in the rough.

Why can't you see it,

Yourself?

Mirroring

The way you look at yourself in the mirror,

I wonder, what goes through your mind?

As you see your beautiful imperfections

And try to accept your insecurities;

All on your own...

Disorganized

How can someone so clean,

Be so disorganized in everything

Pertaining to their life?

We can free flow through some things.

But we can't drift away all the time.

Babble

You must love the sound of your own voice.

Because you never allow me to say a word.

And even when I do speak,

   You talk over me.

As if you know it all.

But, really, you don't know anything.

For once, don't talk – just listen.

Heart

You often show more heart than I do.

And I'm learning through your example.

But, I'm prideful about how

> My heart is being exposed to you.

Indifferent

As we grew aware of our circumstances,

Our situation began to evolve.

Though we continued to be close,

We also began to feel indifferent...

Changes

Changes are inevitable. I just hope you're prepared for them. I never want to alter the person of which you are. But I never want to see your growth or maturity underdeveloped, either...

Compromising

Arguing in-between emotions and logic,

Trying to find a common ground.

We found ourselves:

Compromising,

Swallowing our pride

And understanding,

While still at odds.

Appreciation

I only wish your mouth

Would speak the words

I long for...

"I love you."

"I need you."

"I want you."

"I see you."

"Thank you."

Observing

Soon enough, infatuation faded.

Our rose-tinted glasses came off.

And, we stood staring at reality,

Observing things

We hadn't noticed...

The things that once intrigued us,

Soon became

The very things we began to hate

The most about each other...

Sabotage

Your dark past,

Tends to overshadow

What you're trying to accomplish.

And, before you know it

You're in too deep

Unable to get out of the darkness.

But, instead of asking for help

You dwell there, alone

Thinking nobody notices,

But, oh, I notice...

Quiet Place

When you drift off into

That quiet place in your mind,

I am left alone with questions

You refuse to answer

And a lost soul

Seeking something unknown.

Bartender

You pour your heart out

Like an untrained bartender

Leaving everyone drunken but happy.

Which is the smallest cost to them

But, the biggest debt for yourself...

Ugly

I often wonder

If you notice how ugly

You become when triggered or upset.

I often wonder if you notice

How beautiful you are, even

While you're being so ugly to me.

Liquid Courage

You become another person when you indulge in liquid courage.

Your words are slurred with persuasions. Your voice elevated in volume. Your actions become bolder, and your attitude becomes a rollercoaster with a cautionary disclaimer.

And, I am sobered by experiencing you in such a manner. So damaged by the collateral, your actions bring upon us.

The Rush

It shouldn't take you

This long to get ready.

You knew what was going to happen.

You should've been prepared.

Now, I have to sit here, waiting for you.

Here we go, again!

You're making us late, as always...

Waves

There was no more free flow.

Our vibe began to get choppy.

And, our current situation began to go under,

Experiencing waves of chaotic destruction...

Complications

We dwelt somewhere in-between:

I love you in all the right ways

But, for all the wrong reasons

And

I love you with all the right intentions

But, with no clue of what I am doing

Obligations

When the praise is gone and

There are no words left to be said;

Will our presence be enough

    To sustain what we've made?

When the pleasure is gone and joy has faded;

    Will we still feel the same way?

Everything's becoming an obligation

    Done on behalf of each other,

Instead of a willful act of love

    Provided for one another...

Routine

Over and over, again.

Over and over, again.

Same thing.

Same thing.

Over and over, again.

Over and over, again.

I'm over it...

When will the routine stop

And the fun starts to kick in?

This

I know you mean well.

But, it's hard to believe

> This is it...

> This is us...

Because

> This isn't enough...

Seriously, what's the point?

Loving You

Loving you isn't easy

But I can't seem to walk away

From whatever this is,

We got going...

Soul Cry

Your soul cries out

For all the things it's deprived of

    Love,

    Acceptance,

    Understanding;

And, trust me, I get it.

Honestly, I do.

But, I only wish

You'll find it where you are;

Instead of where you've been

Or where you might go afterward.

Familiar

I've never been one to beg. I've never been one to open up. So there was no reason to lend my heart to a stranger. There was no reason to be vulnerable with a friend.

I didn't trust people. I didn't trust their ways. I knew better than to love. It'd only bring pain. But why does this feel so different? Yet, still the same?

Disappearing

As I walked passed the mirror,

I had to do a double-take.

I couldn't grasp the image.

I couldn't identify who it was.

I had to stare for a moment.

I was in disbelief at what I saw.

That wasn't me.

It wasn't me at all.

Actually, to be honest...

I didn't know who I was anymore...

Still

If I changed,

Would you still,

Love me the same?

Just a Moment

Wanting to feel something for a moment.

Wanting to recall what used to be.

When bad got worse,

    We began to seek:

        Guidance,

        Some sort of justice.

        And fillers for voids.

Just to stop the pain.

Just to remember what it feels like

    To be alive and free...

Hair Down

You learned to let go

    And let your hair down.

But, I wonder if it was

    For the right reason...

Bonfire

Our old phases brought new flames

Into our circle of firewood and twigs.

Leaving us engaged and entertained.

Dancing and exchanging words

With our demons while full of spirits;

Casting our cares into the fire, unscathed.

Fire and Desire

When we met,

I marveled at your speech.

I was captivated by your words.

I evaluated your stance.

I understood your grounding.

I knew what I was getting myself into.

But, I never cared to be cautious.

For what fun is it

To overanalyze fire and desire?

No, you just go with the flow of it.

You Are

To me,

You're a breath of fresh air.

You're a quenched thirst.

To me,

You're food for thought.

You're a needed want.

To me,

You're an answered prayer.

You are.

Risk

I'd risk it all to be with you.

That's the problem.

Temptation

I know that I shouldn't

But I want to.

I know crossing that line is risky

But I can't help it; I want you.

Position

Your invitation turned into a visit. Our bodies disappeared into the darkness. Conscious minds numbed by liquid spirits. Hearts lighting the paths of your apartment.

Our bodies intertwined within a bed of forbidden pleasures. Vices uncovered and exposed. Voices elevating through dusk. Our bodies going through the motions. Our passionate desires die after climax as we resurface. No touching, just vibing off love's current.

Our mistakes haunting us while leaving in the morning. Our actions are evident while questioning our focus. I don't know what we were thinking. I thought I did but, I didn't...Too late to take back what did and didn't happen when in this position, isn't it?

Fix

We never spoke about it again. Instead, we stored it within the attics of our minds.

Our foundation crumbling under pressure. Our bodies ailing from the stress.

There was nothing we could do to fix it. There was nothing I could do to heal us. There was nothing we could do...

We were languishing...

Idol

Swiftly, I tried to detach myself from temptation. Taking sabbaticals, denying myself, and trying to refocus.

I erased your number, though I remembered. I blocked your feed, though I envisioned your image. I even prayed and fasted, though I could shake my craving.

Yet, I swore I was okay and ready to move on. Until I found myself back to my old ways. Dwelling in your presence, again...

With You

When I'm with you,

I am at ease.

When I'm with you,

I am well pleased.

When I'm alone,

I question everything.

Different Angel

With the face of an angelic being

I saw a glimpse of heaven on earth.

But unfortunately,

It wasn't who I thought it was

Once I sobered up...

Games

It was all

Fun and games

Until someone got hurt...

Spirits

When the drinks came,

The truth began to pour out

Quicker than the liquor

Swallowed by loudmouths...

Triggers

I wish I knew

What words triggered you the most

Because, when you gave me that look

I knew that I had messed up severely.

Gamer

You like to push my buttons.

As if I'm plugged into your console.

But, I hate the games you play.

And, this isn't a tournament

I'd like to win, honestly...

Spilling

There were no signs around.

So, I never thought to be cautious.

Until I fell – face first,

Spilling my past into my present...

Bittersweet

Disappointment,

Often leaves

A bittersweet taste

Upon my tongue, still...

Fluid

As water trickles down my eyes,

Liquor seems to hydrate your demons...

Deflecting

When questions arose,

I deflected while rejecting

Everything that was sent my way.

Even I couldn't handle

The truth at that moment.

It was too much to face.

Console

Continuously,

You pushed me away

While I tried to console you.

I tried to hold on.

But, you had let go

Before I could even reach you.

Translations

You used to hang onto every word I'd say.
Now, I often find you drifting off, lost within
the spaces of my sentences. Looking for lost
translations, double meanings, lousy
grammar, and false punctuations.

Burn

You often like to fight - fire with fire;

Leaving us no way to survive.

Only burn in this place, together.

I Knew

Without you saying a word, I knew. I don't know how but I did. It's an unction, a feeling, a vibe. It's a sense, a nudge, a conviction. I can't explain it, but I knew.

Yet, I denied it. I dismissed that intuition. That divine insight, telling me something was wrong. That certain mood, I couldn't shake. That sentiment of constantly feeling and being alone.

I knew, but I had more faith in you than myself. Because I thought you'd be the last person to do me wrong. Crazy, how wrong I was, but I knew...I knew all along

Accident

Incidents occurred.

Accidents happened.

But, when I called you on your BS.

That accident

Caused *permanent* damage,

None of us was ready for.

try

I try to talk to you

But, you have nothing to say.

I call your name,

But, you don't answer me.

I try to understand how you feel

But you say that you're numb.

I tend to draw near

But you're unavailable.

I try to compromise

But, you won't allow me

To meet you where you are.

I show up for you

But you don't seem to care at all.

But, still, I try.

Oh, how I try.

To make an effort, somehow

For this lover of mine.

Roommates

Things began to shift,

As more silence crept in.

And we became strangers

Inside the home we built.

Secrets

My imagination ran rapid.

Slowly drifting downstream.

My insecurities having the best of me.

My past resurfacing.

Damning traumas

     Leaving me broken,

     Doubting myself,

     Ignoring my instincts,

     Blaming myself,

     Forgetting accountability;

All because

     We changed. You changed. I changed.

Loud House

Your quiet soul began to scream.

Louder and louder, it cried out.

Begging for answers.

Pleading for release.

Hoping for healing.

And praying for me.

Unwanted

You don't look at me as you used to.

It's like,

    No one is home.

    The lights are off.

    The rooms are cold

And there's no way for me to stay

Because I'm not welcomed

Here, any longer.

Reason

As we dwelt together but alone;

Hurting for different reasons.

I understood, I caused –

Unforgivable pain,

Unfortunate suffering,

Undeniable trauma,

Unnecessary drama,

For no valid reason, rather than to

Hide my own fears and insecurities

With momentary pleasures.

Prisoner

I feel like a prisoner within my body

As we both continue to treat each other

Like we're dangerous strangers

Instead of each other's person.

Freedom

Released into a new profound freedom

I exercised my right to:

Forget the rules,

Feel the most,

And, do what was best for me;

Regardless of the consequences...

Serious

It didn't dawn on me how serious

The reality of this situation was

Until I saw you leaving with

The biggest piece of me,

My heart;

Dysfunctional

Nothing seemed to matter.

Nothing seemed to work.

We dwelt together in dysfunction,

Praying for a way through

And an easy way out.

Mirrored

It wasn't long

Before I began to

Mirror the image

You presented to me.

Prize

You began to take more than you could give.

As if:

You needed a reward to be present

Or

Wanted a prize to stay put.

Prideful

I miss you, but I can't tell you.

I love you, but I can't express it.

I need you, but you don't know it.

I messed up...I admit it.

To myself, of course...

Support

I tried to pick up the pieces

Of what I had broken but,

You had already started to rebuild

Yourself without me

I guess you didn't need

My help or support, after all...

Voice Mail

After a while,

Your voicemail was the only way

I could hear your voice.

I left multiple messages,

Hoping you'd listen to one.

But, my truth was the last thing

You wanted to hear and, honestly;

I don't blame you at all...

House & Home

This home was full of laughter.

Four walls holding conversations.

Every side was heard and considered.

Lights were always left on,

   As we dwelt within.

But, this home soon became a house,

   The longer you stayed away.

Silence crept in

   And emotions took up residence.

Kicking out joy, decayed happiness;

We lost everything we dreamt of

   While burning bridges.

Lost Cause

The smallest impact created the biggest ripple. Causing eyes to open and feelings to change. Yet, slowly everything we built stood incomplete.

My heart began to hide behind walls of insecurities, and your mind began to attract fault. While your spirit reasoned with your emotions, my acceptance of flaws battled with accountability clauses.

It left me stripped of everything I've known, Including your hope, love, and forgiveness. It was like I was locked out of heaven's doors. Just a lost cause, wandering, again.

Familiar Stranger

Sitting in silence,

Staring at a familiar stranger,

That had nothing to say.

I came to a conclusion,

I'm losing myself...

I'm losing myself, again.

Hypocrites

We became the same people

We swore we never wanted to become.

And did all of the things

We swore we never wanted to do.

Solitude

Months passed by

As we changed like the seasons

Our Eden feelings were

Dead from winter's harshness.

I found myself sprung off the heat

From what I could remember,

Instead of the chill I experienced daily.

Only the emptiness I felt

And the silence I heard after,

Gifted me guilt and shame

For constantly reminiscing

Over past happenings.

In Love

To make matters worse,

Even after taking a break,

I still found myself in love

Even within this mess, you made...

Messy

I didn't ask for this to happen.

I didn't know you'd walk into my life

    And flip my world upside down.

You went through my life,

    Seeking a place to belong;

Opening the doors to the

    Chambers of my heart,

Only to expose a part of myself

    That was hidden for so long;

Even I didn't know what to do

    When my baggage was tossed

    Upon the floor of my soul;

And the skeletons that hung

    Within my mind were now

    Spilling out into the open, visible.

I was stunned, scared, shocked;

Pissed – to say the least...

I had to send you on your way

    As I was left with the mess

    We made out of love.

Unraveled

You unraveled my heartstrings

　　　As you left me here, alone;

Holding a bloody ball of yawn;

While you went out to find

Something entertaining to string along...

Options

Wracking my brain, I weighed my options. I counted the cost. I made notes of my assets and liabilities. I prayed to God for signs and wonders. I sat, and I observed. I questioned myself.

Yet, when I looked around, I saw too much damage. Damage that memories and promises couldn't salvage.

An invisible expectation lingered, leaving me unsure we'd make it back to where we came from. And I didn't know if I wanted to go back or if moving forward was the best option for me...

Decisions

Sometimes,

All you can do is pray

That you made the best decision

And accept the fact,

There's a chance that it is or isn't.

Calling

When you called,

I was hesitant to answer.

Unsure of what would be said,

Uncertain of how it'll be taken.

But you called, and I answered.

Like a fool, I fell for it again.

But this time, I was glad I did.

This time, I had something to say.

The Return

When you walked through my door,

I was glad to see you again.

Yet, to my surprise,

You stood with a different demeanor

You embodied

A new profound strength,

Something,

I hadn't seen in you, before

Fear of God

I found myself dumbfounded,

Unable to speak

Within your presence.

The fire in your eyes,

Set my body ablaze.

As I beheld your glory,

And felt the wrath you held in.

I knew things were different,

But, I wasn't ready for such a change.

Questioning

Can we talk about it or

Should we just leave it alone?

Is this real, or are we

Pretending with one another?

Broken or well put together,

Can we trust our hearts?

Our mind's full of questions but,

Our mouths won't speak those emotions.

Elephant

We were openly vulnerable.

Speaking up.

Exposing our experiences.

Revealing everything on our minds,

Instead of hiding,

The elephant in the room or

Walking on peanut shells.

We aired out our dirty laundry

And let the animal roam freely

For a change.

Flawed

I saw your compelling potential.

I knew what you were capable of.

And, I took a chance on you.

Now, look at what we've become.

Stay

When I came around,

You needed me to stay.

When you came around,

I wanted you to stay.

There was always a difference between us, but I thought we could look passed it. I thought our vision of love was more significant than the minor details hidden in the bigger picture...

Earned

You asked what I wanted and needed.

You learned what I liked and disliked.

You knew what I had to offer.

Yet, you expected more from me

Than what you were willing to

Put in or give back yourself.

I did the work, and you took the credit;

    For everything we formed,

    And everything we made here.

As if we didn't build this.

As if we didn't create this – together.

Sorry

How do you say, "I'm sorry."

When words and actions

Just aren't enough

Do you say it or act it out?

Do you forget about it?

Do you just move on?

How do you say...

"I'm sorry..."

I really am sorry, love...

Abandoned

There's a part of me that questions if you'll show up for me or leave me — like I've done you, in the past...

Left

I waited for you to circle back around.

I was standing alone – in the dark.

But, to my surprise, you never returned.

You left – you left me there, by myself...

Boundary

There had to be a line between

YOURS | **MINE** | <u>OURS</u>

Were

When your body wandered,

Your mind forgot who you were.

When your eyes wandered,

Your hands didn't stay where they were.

When your hands wandered,

Your heart forgot whose you were.

When your spirit remembered,

Your soul couldn't take the remorse.

When you returned home,

Your reflection was all you had left.

Project

Your mind became busy.

Your hands went to work.

As soon as your eyes spotted a new project.

As soon as you fell in love with another side

   Of me.

Excuses

I do love you.

I'd do anything for you.

But, there are things you should know.

And, things you should understand...

My eyes can't help what they fall upon.

My body can't stop what it feels.

I'm me!

I have needs and desires.

I'm human!

I can't help it.

Fear

You don't have to fear the unknown.
Instead, Fear only what is known by you.

For there is a greater chance for things to
happen because, what you know, you'll do.

Mess

I dwelt in-between my love for you

And the betrayal you brought to me.

Even in the midst of this mess of love

I still had to do what was best for me.

Fantasy

My love waxed cold.

My thoughts grew dark.

My dream turned into a nightmare,

    As I tried to gain control of life;

My love was gone.

My blood boiled.

My dream now fading,

    As I tried to gain back

The proper visual of my self-image,

Instead of my fantasies expectations.

Silent Treatment

Your silence left me uneasy as you chose to:

Quiet your truth,

Dismiss your thoughts,

Reject your feelings,

And, distance yourself

You said it was to protect yourself.

But, really, it was to punish me, too.

Our safe space turned dangerously silent.

It's not hard to notice.

Just read the room...

Own It

Let's be serious.

It's not about being right or wrong.

I just want you to:

    Identify the problem.

    If you did it, own it!

    Learn how to solve it, together.

    Instead of being at odds, apart.

It's just that simple.

But you don't get it.

You can't own up to it...

Force of Love

You can't force love

To like you.

You can't force likeliness

To love you.

Sweet Nothings

I refuse to be ignorant.

I refuse to be naïve.

I just wonder how many people

You whisper sweet nothings to

As if they're the only one

You're talking too...

Them

The way you talk about them,

I wonder why you're still here with me...

Them, Again

You craved something I couldn't give.

You wanted someone I couldn't be.

You loved someone that wasn't me.

You needed who they were,

Not who I am at the moment.

And, that's alright.

But you could've told me.

You should've said,

You wanted them all along.

ame

Although, they are gorgeous – I'll admit it; I still can't get over how you look at us the same.

I noticed the way your eyes are set aflame by their sparks. They must be someone special because you used to do the same for me.

It's a poignant observation, I cannot ignore anymore. Although, it hurts like hell to admit. I'll learn to be happy for you. For them. For y'all...

Either Or

I can be

      The person you hate

      Or

      The person you love.

However,

      I cannot be

      And

      Will not be both.

Influence

Even in the midst

Of our most challenging moments,

You still push me to become

A better version of myself,

As if you still see potential in me

That I can't...

Reflecting

Looking into your eyes,

All I could see was my reflection.

As if nobody had been allowed

That deep inside you, but me...

The Art of Letting Go

If I'm not the one

Will you let me go?

I know it's hard for you

But, it might be right for us.

If I'm not the one

Why are we holding on?

Release the strings of my heart

So I can be free to move along...

Forever

Don't promise me forever.

It's much too far away.

From the place where we're present.

From the time of which we've been.

Don't promise me forever.

You don't mean what you say.

Honestly, how could you?

You've never experienced

Forever with someone.

Being consumed by their being.

Being immersed in their current.

Waiting for eternity to emanate

Their new beginnings.

Waiting for the chance

That you were told would come.

Don't promise me forever.

And, if you feel those words

Fumble upon your tongue;

Spit out the exact opposite

Of the words you desire to mouth.

Don't release your lies upon my mind.

Don't lay your promises upon my heart.

Forever isn't promised;

We never know how it'll turn out.

Don't promise me forever.

Don't fill me with your doubt.

Me, don't promise forever.

Forever, don't promise me – at all.

Joker

I dealt you a hand. And by the looks of you, I knew where I stood. Placing my cards upon the table, I told you, "Stop playing. Give up while you still can." I knew you had lost it all in that moment, and I was okay with that. Although, we were both bluffing; I knew this was the last gamble for us.

Confessions

I admit it.

I do love you.

But I also dislike you, just the same.

It's just that love

Tends to overpower my hate...

Alone

And when you tell me

You're leaving,

I usually want to beg you

To stay.

However, I know,

You must go

And, I must learn

How to be alone, again.

The Breakup

And it was over, just like that. A straightforward conversation ended everything we'd known and built.

As we began sorting through our pain – cutting ties and returning each other's pieces; a door was opened for us. There the future stood in front of us, waiting.

And it was so different from what we had expected. But, we made peace with it while leaving the past behind. We left our love broken. Yet, walked into the future – alone and single, but whole again.

The Cost

I guess they weren't lying,

When they said:

It'll only take.

     A quick moment.

     An innocent thought.

     A lapse of judgment.

It'll only take.

     A desirable choice.

     A sudden urge.

     A delayed reaction.

It'll only take.

A swift motion.

A single word.

That one person.

It'll only take.

Yeah, it'll only take.

It'll only cost you

    EVERYTHING...

Turn Around

I might've turned around to see if my perception was clear. Checking if I missed something or if you were watching me leave. Hoping you were contemplating staying behind or running towards me, but you weren't there.

It's like all that I knew was a mirage. An illusion I created to protect myself and preserve your self-image, but the potential wasn't enough. We both became victims of this illusion and stopped showing up in reality.

Yet, the pang of guilt left as relief washed over me. At that moment, the revelation I knew came into fruition – It was over. The narrative ended. The illusion fell apart. My intuition was right. You were never really there, to begin with, and neither was I.

Before

I never tried to run after you.

The chase ended before it began.

When you walked away

I could finally catch my breath.

And, before you were gone;

I noticed I had already left.

Letting Go of Holding On

It's never easy to let go

But,

It's never easy to hold on

Either.

Afterward

After the breakup,

I tried to regroup.

Turning back to my old habits,

I did what I wanted.

I said what I needed to.

Yet, I was still lost in a strange world,

    Afterward,

    After us,

    After you...

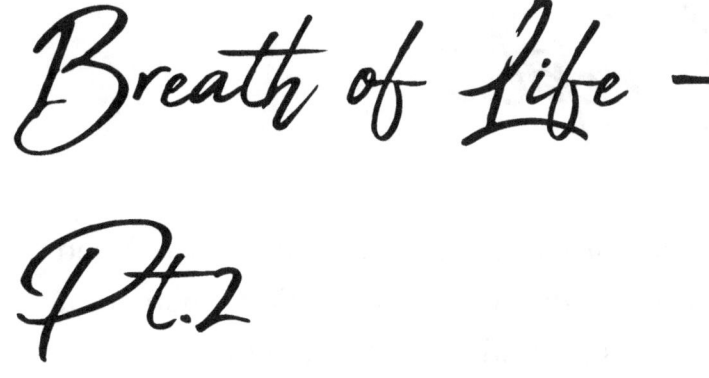

Breath of Life – Pt.2

After letting go of all we had,

I began seeking healing

While learning too:

BREATHE,

Inhaling, *freedom*

And

Exhaling, *acceptance*

Of self

Skeptic

When confronted by our friends, I refused to comply with their interrogation. Instead of making up an alibi, I objected the accusations – claiming everything was fine between us.

When testifying of our past, I swore that everything was good. Under oath, I said our love was worth it, although my heart swung like a pendulum.

Like a jury full of skeptics, I began to question myself. Then, while becoming a prisoner to my own uncertainty and a judge of my unforgiving sentencing, I began to plead the fifth.

After Awhile

It'll only hurt for a little while.

For a while, you'll feel the burn.

Then, the sting will subside.

Yes, after a while, you won't remember.

The pain will gradually leave.

And, after a while,

    You won't remember this at all...

Love's Hangover

You don't want to know what I did. You don't want to know how I survived.

Baby, I danced with a couple of people. I flirted with folks at parties. I conversed with individuals on rooftops. I traveled with my companions to places I'd never been before.

I drank a lot of shots and got drunk. I numbed the hurt I felt to the beat of my favorite songs. I attracted beautiful beings whose names I did not know. I captured a couple of hearts and left a few broken with only pictures to show.

I puked the pain of betrayal. I cried about my situation and circumstances. I vented to my family, and I cussed amongst friends. I poured out my heart. I prayed away the agony. I repented for my sins. I changed the things I did.

Yet, even after all of that...I couldn't wash away your essence from my skin. I couldn't erase your memory from my mind. I couldn't unravel our heartstrings – Undoing what you did, I did, and we did. You and me, us, and them...

So, as I faced the mirror, all of those mornings. Hungover, disgusted, and distorted. I forced myself to face reality because it is what it is, and it isn't what it isn't.

Grief

It is okay for you to cry – release the pain.
Forgive yourself for the trust given, faith had,
and all that's lost.

It is okay for you to feel – release the hurt.
Mourn the loss of the moments lived,
Memories created, Dreams made, and time
spent.

It is okay that things didn't work out. I
promise you, it is. You can mourn the loss
but, remember you have to rise from the
ashes afterward.

Remembrance

I loved you,

Those feelings don't fade.

Your memory hasn't been erased.

Your name hasn't become

Bitter upon my lips

Or left unspoken.

Instead, it's a reminder of

What did and didn't happen.

I loved you,

Those feelings don't disappear.

It is forever instilled in my heart,

Connected to the eternal source

Through prayer, for reconciliation

And Repentance of lost causes

I loved you.

And, that's okay.

Even if that love wasn't

What I thought it'd be.

It was an experience that brought me

Closer to finding the real thing.

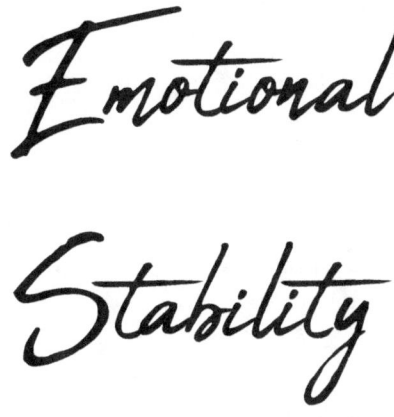

Emotional Stability

While you're hurting,

They're possibly feeling nothing at all.

While you're obsessing,

They're out, doing what they want.

While you're stressing,

They're living their best life.

Relax, don't trip.

Do you and watch, they'll notice.

Rumors

Rumors spread like wildfire.

My ears ringing from the sirens,

Singing the lullaby of anguish,

Luring me into their presence.

I stopped and listened,

Hypnotized by their melody

I'd fallen victim to their song.

While reopening the wounds of my heart.

After Me

I forgot.

After me,

There would be more...

Mourning Reports

It's hard to move on and

Genuinely be happy for someone,

When their happiness is

Constantly reported to you

During your mourning process...

Stories & Details

I heard all kinds of stories.

Things that left me up in arms.

Things that made me question:

 What was I fighting for?

 What was I waiting on?

 And, what was I seeking after?

The Others

There's always going to be another;

That will swing by or lend a hand.

But,

There will only be one – forever;

That'll stay and hold your sentiment.

Wondering

I wonder —who they are.

The person whose name you speak so effortlessly. It rolls off your tongue like you've said it a million times. Maybe you have. Maybe, they're the one you talk to, revealing the hidden emotion behind your silent treatments.

I wonder – do they listen?

The person whose ear now has the words you speak so effortlessly. It's possible; they've heard you vent a billion times. Maybe they have. Maybe, they're the person you communicate with. Possibly, that's where my time, texts, and phone calls went. They were spent with them.

I wonder – do they know about me?

The person who's been here for you,
working through everything; Have I been
brought up in your conversations as
effortlessly? Has my name slipped from
your lips just like theirs? Maybe it has.
Maybe, but that's something I'll never know
at this point.

But, I wonder...

Difference

I'm trying to Distinguish

The difference between:

Being on my own, alone

And

Experiencing loneliness without you

They both seem the same but,

One is because of my choice

And

One is because of your choice

Questioning Again

And, I know that I should be happy.

Don't get me wrong, I am, to some degree...

However, I just can't help but question;

What was wrong –

    With us?

    With you?

    With me?

Unanswered

I often wonder,

Do you think about me anymore?

But that's a question

I'm not sure I want to be answered...

Afraid

I'd be a liar

If I didn't confess

I'm afraid of my heart

Being toyed with and

My soul being crushed

By myself or any other person, again.

Yourself

I only wish that

You needed me,

Just as much as

You needed yourself, too.

Sacrifices

I would've given you everything,

If you asked;

But, what would I have been left with,

If I did?

Future Pains

It pains me to know that

You'll be someone else's:

    Friend or lover,

    Fiancé or Spouse

    Or even a parent.

And I will only be:

    A distant memory,

    A faded picture,

    A forgotten love,

    And, a stranger...

Honest Healing

I'm jealous of who has your attention.
Envious of who's taking up the majority of
your time.

I'm angered about who's getting closer to
you. Saddened about how it's stealing away
your heart.

I'm numbed by the conversations being had
about the future. A little shocked; you're
moving on so fast.

I'm happy you're doing so well but bitter
that it's happening without me. I miss you,
but I dare not say it aloud.

Because this is the process of healing from
heartbreak alone...

Moving On

I hope they're everything that I never was.

So, you'll have a reason to remember me

And a reason to move on without.

Memories

Sometimes, I'm reminded of you.

Captivated by those

Pristine glimpses of what was.

Sometimes, I think of you,

And our days of wild glory;

Sometimes, I want to see you

Present in my life

But, for now, my mind will have to do.

The memories are enough,

Until I'm truly over you...

Wrong

I guess it's possible to love someone:

    In all the wrong ways,

    For all the wrong reasons,

    During all the wrong seasons,

    And at the wrong timing,

    But, to the best of your abilities,

Unfortunately...

The Hardest Part

The hardest part of all of this

Is accepting the truth

    And ignoring the denial.

I know you won't walk through the door.

I know you won't come back home.

I know that you've moved on but,

Whenever the phone rings,

A part of me still hopes that

It's you...

Deja vu

It all feels so familiar

Like I've done this before

Or I've been in this moment, previously...

Crossed Paths

Walking around aimless, I escaped the rush to clear my mind. Inhaling life's unknown, I exhaled my expectations.

Wandering the city's streets, I window-shopped amongst the crowds while nestled in my comfort and settled into my new reality — along the way.

Yet, accidentally, I crossed a path that led me to bump into you again...

 Welcoming

Funny, bumping into you again, you said you'd never return. Crazy how time flies by, and we become hypocrites of foolish words. I'm not surprised. It's been a while, after all.

It seems like no one can resist the city lights. And no one can escape the core of its heart.

Funny how things turned out for us. I said you'd come back. Crazy how time flies by, and we become curious about the things we lost. I'm not surprised. I knew I'd see you again, after all.

It seems like no one can resist the place they've called home. And, no one can escape that sort of attraction to true love.

Honestly...this time, I hope you find what you are looking for. You deserve a place where you can dwell and belong. You deserve a place to settle down and call your

own. So, welcome back, stranger; Welcome
home.

Complicated

I saw you around. We spoke every now and again, acting as if nothing had happened. We'd bypass each other's glares. We'd smile and wave off the feels.

But, the last time was different.

When you called out my name, it stopped me for a second. I continued, trying to disregard your voice, only to be taken aback when you spun me around.

Looking into your eyes, you seemed concerned. I knew that look but said nothing as you asked how I was. I pulled away as I responded with a shaky whisper,

"It's complicated..."

 Conscious

If this has taught you anything,

It should've made you:

Aware of what you have

And

Mindful of what you loss

In this world, it's all — give and take.

Everything has a cost.

So, what do you have to offer now?

Comprehend

Honestly, one day – you will know.

I had so much love for you;

But, you couldn't comprehend

The full magnitude...

Just Enough

You loved me,

The only way you knew how.

Imperfectly perfect,

Giving me the little you had.

Which seemed like a lot to you;

During your life lessons

    And constant pursuit

    of achieving some type of happiness.

And it was just enough.

Just enough to change the two of us,

Forever...

Forgiveness

I know you're not ready to meet yet.

I know talking is not an option.

I know, your heart is currently healing;

But, over time, I hope you know;

I didn't mean you any harm.

Although I did hurt you...

I'm sorry.

Please forgive me.

I love you.

Bond

No love lost,

Just a heartbreak

Between two bonded souls.

Breaking

Sometimes,

We tend to break our own hearts,

Instead of others...

Broken

I don't regret what we were or currently are. That's what we were supposed to be.

See, it took some time for me to grasp that all I wanted to do was assist you when it came to healing what was hurting.

And, I guess, in a twisted way, this was necessary because I never could've fixed what was broken inside you. You have to do that on your own.

Space

I know not what I'm capable of.

All I know is what I currently am.

And that is enough for me to fight

For whatever it is, I'm becoming

Whether we're

Together, Distant, or Apart

On Your Own

Sometimes,

The only way to truly love a person

is by letting them go, heal and learn

On their own.

Adventure Time

I'm ready for a vacation.

A small break from my daily routine.

A little adventure that I could enjoy.

Anything to take my mind off

    of what had occurred.

Everything that could help me not

Remember what didn't occur.

I needed something positive

To come out of this with me...

Arrival

Surrounded by many places, observing a few views; I dabbled in a few bodies of water. I swam and grew acquainted with some places I had explored, too.

I learned their names and capitals. I admired their culture and history. The people touched my heart deeply but, none of them intrigued me like you.

So, after many memories and connections were made, I waited patiently – whole yet, still healing. I headed home, alone – where I needed to find my own comfort. I dwelt there awhile, contemplating what to do. That's where I learned to just be – without you.

Over

Delete the number.

Erase the pictures.

Block the profiles.

Log off everything.

Until you're ready to return,

Don't torture yourself.

Acknowledge you're hurting.

Embrace the pain.

Accept the fact that it's over.

It's really over.

Ghost

You called yesterday and heard

(I'm sorry, but the number you have reached
has been disconnected. Goodbye.)

You swung by my place and learned

(I'm sorry, nobody by that name lives here
any longer.)

You checked social media and found

(Sorry this page is unavailable.

Sorry that page doesn't exist!

This page isn't available.

There's nothing here.)

You sent an email and saw

(A message that you sent could not be delivered to one or more of its recipients.)

Even an IM

(Username is offline.)

Now, it's like you're haunted by me. You can't find a trace of me anywhere except where I've always been, constantly in your heart and mind.

Release

And, I release myself

From the responsibility of:

    Loving you as a spouse,

    Providing for you as a fiancé,

    Caring for you as a lover,

    Protecting you as a best friend,

    Knowing you as a friend,

I tried my best, being everything

    I could have and could not have been.

But now, we're returning back

    To the state of being acquaintance;

    Strangers, again

Late — Pt.3

It might take me a moment to catch my breath, but next time, I won't rush to get where I'm supposed to go.

No. Instead, I'll arrive when it's time and wait patiently for my perfect moment. I'll enjoy the journey to my destination while observing all that life has to offer along the way.

Because it's okay to be human. It's okay to just be. To slow down and stop to observe the world around you. It's okay to be early or even late. You're allowed to pick your pace.

Yes. Sometimes, you don't need to rush. Just wait, love.

Well Wishes

I still wish you all the

Love and happiness

Of which you deserve

Even if it's not with me

But, with somebody else

Or even yourself

I can't believe I'm saying this

But, I had to wish you well...

Thinking Out Loud

Damnit!

My mind

Is speaking to

My heart, again...

About The Author

Kid Gillis - A Twenty-eight year old, outspoken writer and content creator is here to make a beautiful mess of things.

This New York City based artist aims to use what she has to help others and give back something creatively ingenious to enjoy.

The young visionary has gained hands-on experience while living, learning, and working within her craft field. In addition, she has dedicated herself to documenting, creating, and capturing human experiences through various creative forms.

Get Connected:

If you'd like to learn more about Kid Gillis and the projects she is currently working on, visit the links below!

OFFICIAL WEBSITE:

WWW.KIDGILLIS.COM

TWITTER:

WWW.TWITTER.COM/KIDGILLIS

INSTAGRAM:

WWW.INSTAGRAM.COM/KIDGILLIS

FACEBOOK:

WWW.FACEBOOK.COM/KIDGILLIS

www.ingramcontent.com/pod-product-compliance
Lightning Source LLC
Chambersburg PA
CBHW050921030726
47503CB00007BB/2410